DreamWorks
HOW TO TRAIN YOUR
DRAGON
THE HIDDEN WORLD

WORLD OF DRAGONS

ILLUSTRATED BY
PATRICK SPAZIANTE

BY
MAY NAKAMURA

Simon Spotlight
New York   London   Toronto   Sydney   New Delhi

THE DRAGONS

WELCOME TO THE HIDDEN WORLD

You may have heard of an old sailor's tale—the legend of a Hidden World. It is the ancestral home of all dragons, tucked away underground and beyond the edge of the sea. In this land, thousands of dragons live together in a vast and harmonious world.

Many a sailor has searched for this magical kingdom, never to return. Some say that they fell into the sunset or off the edge of the earth. The sailors who did return told stories of dragons guarding the entrance to a great waterfall. No Viking has laid eyes on the Hidden World . . . until now.

Look around closely. Take in the sights that so few human eyes have witnessed before you: a world stretching farther than you can see. . . . Prepare to meet every dragon type that has ever crossed a Viking's path.

Behold: the Hidden World of dragons!

A GUIDE TO THE NUMBERS

Many years ago, a Viking named Bork the Bold (also known as Bork the Very, Very Unfortunate) created the **Book of Dragons** to document everything he knew about these mighty creatures. He also developed a system to measure each dragon's unique strengths and abilities. Bork started by gathering all the information he could glean about the legendary Night Fury: its speed, fire-power, jaw strength, and more. Then he used the Night Fury's statistics as a baseline for measuring the other dragons' abilities.

The **Book of Dragons** became a monumental tome for the Vikings. Today, Bork's system is the established method for recording the dragons' fascinating powers.

A GUIDE TO THE DRAGONS' SIZES

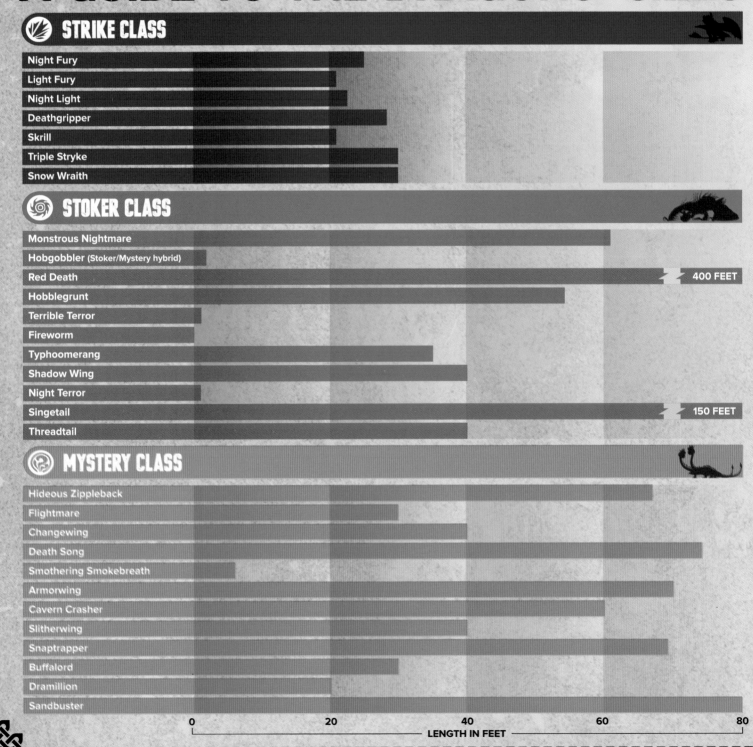

STRIKE CLASS

- Night Fury
- Light Fury
- Night Light
- Deathgripper
- Skrill
- Triple Stryke
- Snow Wraith

STOKER CLASS

- Monstrous Nightmare
- Hobgobbler (Stoker/Mystery hybrid)
- Red Death — 400 FEET
- Hobblegrunt
- Terrible Terror
- Fireworm
- Typhoomerang
- Shadow Wing
- Night Terror
- Singetail — 150 FEET
- Threadtail

MYSTERY CLASS

- Hideous Zippleback
- Flightmare
- Changewing
- Death Song
- Smothering Smokebreath
- Armorwing
- Cavern Crasher
- Slitherwing
- Snaptrapper
- Buffalord
- Dramillion
- Sandbuster

0   20   40   60   80

LENGTH IN FEET

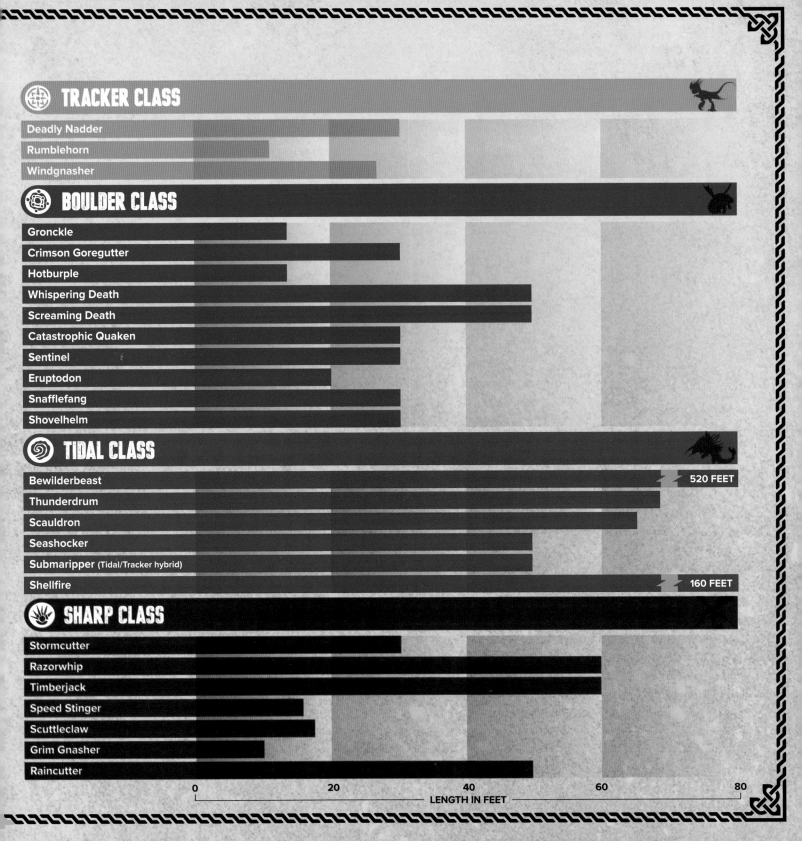

TRACKER CLASS

- Deadly Nadder
- Rumblehorn
- Windgnasher

BOULDER CLASS

- Gronckle
- Crimson Goregutter
- Hotburple
- Whispering Death
- Screaming Death
- Catastrophic Quaken
- Sentinel
- Eruptodon
- Snafflefang
- Shovelhelm

TIDAL CLASS

- Bewilderbeast — 520 FEET
- Thunderdrum
- Scauldron
- Seashocker
- Submaripper (Tidal/Tracker hybrid)
- Shellfire — 160 FEET

SHARP CLASS

- Stormcutter
- Razorwhip
- Timberjack
- Speed Stinger
- Scuttleclaw
- Grim Gnasher
- Raincutter

0   20   40   60   80

LENGTH IN FEET

STRIKE CLASS

Supersonic speed. Silent stealth. Strike Class dragons are the most powerful—and most famous—type of dragon to roam the earth.

Night Fury
FAST AND FEARLESS ALPHA DRAGON

LENGTH: 26 ft	WINGSPAN: 45 ft	WEIGHT: 1,776 lbs

ATTACK	15	
SPEED	20	
ARMOR	18	
FIREPOWER	14	
SHOT LIMIT	6	
VENOM	0	
JAW STRENGTH	6	
STEALTH	18	

Abilities: dive-bombing, blasting plasma, flying at supersonic speeds, navigating in the dark by using echolocation

Personality: fiercely loyal, intelligent

Other facts: Night Furies are the fastest dragons in the sky, along with Light Furies.

Light Fury

IRIDESCENCE IN THE SKY

LENGTH: 22 ft	WINGSPAN: 42 ft	WEIGHT: 1,600 lbs

Stat		Value
ATTACK		15
SPEED		20
ARMOR		18
FIREPOWER		14
SHOT LIMIT		6
VENOM		0
JAW STRENGTH		6
STEALTH		18

Abilities: superheating the trace silicates in their iridescent skin, temporarily making their scales mirrorlike and essentially turning them invisible

Personality: shy, empathetic

Other facts: Just like Night Furies blend into the night sky, Light Furies can easily hide among the clouds and sky during daylight.

Night Light
ADORABLE OFFSPRING OF THE
NIGHT FURY AND THE LIGHT FURY

LENGTH: up to 24 ft	WINGSPAN: up to 44 ft	WEIGHT: up to 1,700 lbs

ATTACK		15*
SPEED		20*
ARMOR		18*
FIREPOWER		14*
SHOT LIMIT		6*
VENOM		0
JAW STRENGTH		6*
STEALTH		18*

*adult Night Lights

Abilities: cloaking themselves by using their own fire blasts to transform their scales into mirrorlike reflectors

Personality: playful and curious

Other facts: Just like the Night Fury and the Light Fury, Night Lights have retractable teeth.

Deathgripper UNBRIDLED DRAGON KILLERS

LENGTH: 28 ft	WINGSPAN: 32 ft	WEIGHT: 2,100 lbs

Stat		Value
ATTACK		27
SPEED		12
ARMOR		20
FIREPOWER		12
SHOT LIMIT		8
VENOM		12
JAW STRENGTH		16
STEALTH		6

Abilities: hunting Vikings *and* dragons, attacking with their tusks and pincers, striking with their poisonous clubbed tail

Personality: brutal

Other facts: Deathgrippers have a fascinating control over their own venom. One strike from a Deathgripper's tail paralyzes its prey. A second strike puts it out of its misery. A third strike makes the body of the prey poisonous to the touch!

Skrill POSITIVELY ELECTRIC

LENGTH: 22 ft	WINGSPAN: 40 ft	WEIGHT: 1,800 lbs

ATTACK	⊕	**14**
SPEED	🪶	**11** 19 on lightning
ARMOR		**10**
FIREPOWER	🔥	**12**
SHOT LIMIT	⚡	**4**
VENOM	💀	**0**
JAW STRENGTH	💎	**5**
STEALTH	▤	**18**

Abilities: channeling lightning along their metallic spines and firing it from their mouths in a showery blast of destruction

Personality: unpredictable, aggressive

Other facts: Skrills cannot fire their lightning strikes from the water.

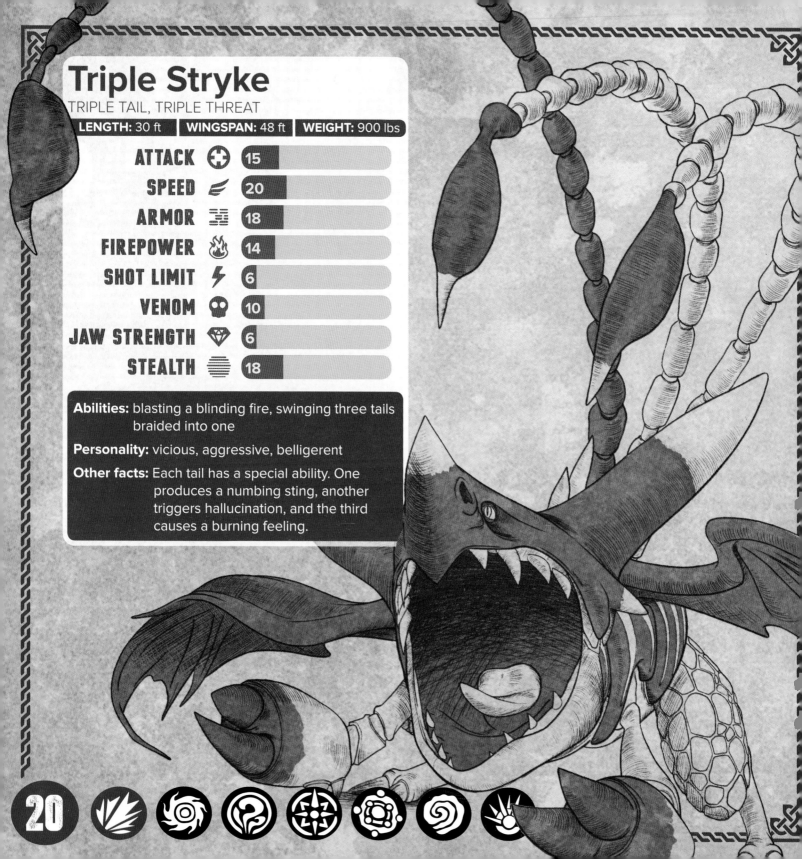

Triple Stryke
TRIPLE TAIL, TRIPLE THREAT

LENGTH: 30 ft	WINGSPAN: 48 ft	WEIGHT: 900 lbs

ATTACK	⊕	15
SPEED	🪶	20
ARMOR	▦	18
FIREPOWER	🔥	14
SHOT LIMIT	⚡	6
VENOM	💀	10
JAW STRENGTH	◈	6
STEALTH	⬙	18

Abilities: blasting a blinding fire, swinging three tails braided into one

Personality: vicious, aggressive, belligerent

Other facts: Each tail has a special ability. One produces a numbing sting, another triggers hallucination, and the third causes a burning feeling.

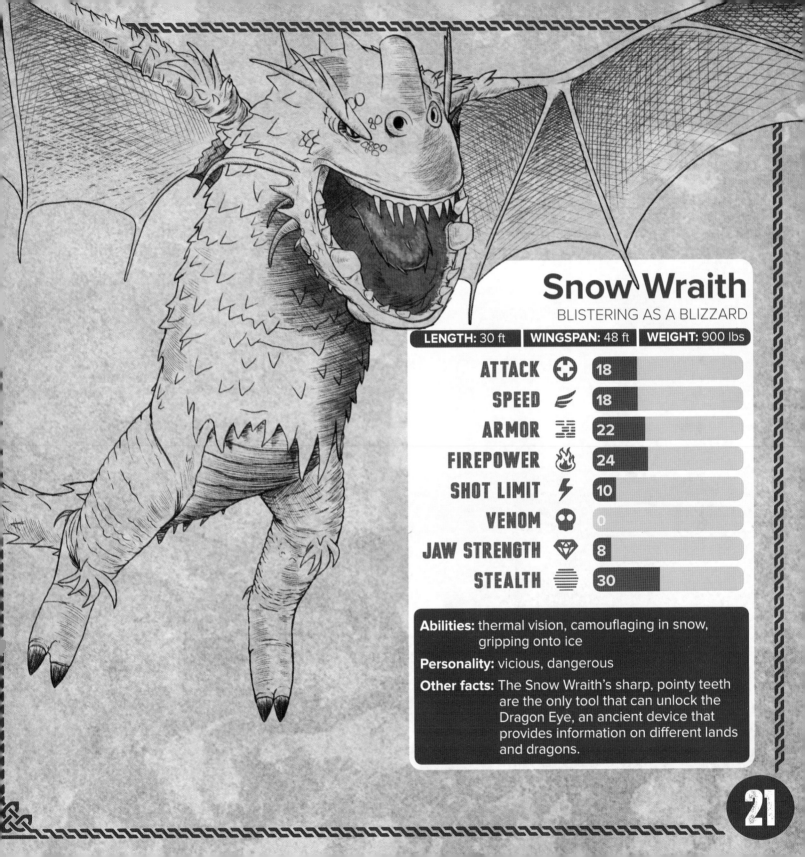

Snow Wraith

BLISTERING AS A BLIZZARD

LENGTH: 30 ft	WINGSPAN: 48 ft	WEIGHT: 900 lbs

Stat		Value
ATTACK	✛	18
SPEED	✦	18
ARMOR	⧉	22
FIREPOWER	🔥	24
SHOT LIMIT	⚡	10
VENOM	💀	0
JAW STRENGTH	💎	8
STEALTH	◉	30

Abilities: thermal vision, camouflaging in snow, gripping onto ice

Personality: vicious, dangerous

Other facts: The Snow Wraith's sharp, pointy teeth are the only tool that can unlock the Dragon Eye, an ancient device that provides information on different lands and dragons.

21

Monstrous Nightmare

THIS DRAGON IS ON FIRE!

LENGTH: 61 ft	**WINGSPAN:** 68 ft	**WEIGHT:** 5,040 lbs

ATTACK		15
SPEED		16
ARMOR		12
FIREPOWER		15
SHOT LIMIT		10
VENOM		0
JAW STRENGTH		6
STEALTH		9

Abilities: self-immolating (covering their body with fire)

Personality: impulsive, easily agitated

Other facts: Monstrous Nightmares light themselves on fire by emitting kerosene from their pores, then breathing fire to set it all aflame.

CLASS: STOKER/MYSTERY HYBRID

Hobgobbler
SMALL OMENS OF BAD LUCK

LENGTH: 3 ft	WINGSPAN: 2 1/2 ft	WEIGHT: 55 lbs

ATTACK		8
SPEED		8
ARMOR		4
FIREPOWER		6
SHOT LIMIT		28
VENOM		0
JAW STRENGTH		12
STEALTH		18

Abilities: devouring everything in their path, attacking in packs

Personality: adorably annoying

Other facts: Hobgobblers can cover their own bodies in super-slick drool to slip out of tight spots.

Red Death QUEEN OF THE DRAGONS

LENGTH: 400 ft	WINGSPAN: 320 ft	WEIGHT: 10 tons (20,000 lbs)

ATTACK 28

SPEED 7

ARMOR 30

FIREPOWER 27

SHOT LIMIT 9

VENOM 0

JAW STRENGTH 22

STEALTH 2

Abilities: commanding other smaller dragons to bring it a constant supply of food, and emitting a homing signal that summons the dragons to its lava-based nest

Personality: commanding

Other facts: Red Deaths have six eyes and no blind spots.

Hobblegrunt

SOOTHING SENSOR

LENGTH: 55 ft | **WINGSPAN:** 63 ft | **WEIGHT:** 4,459 lbs

ATTACK	⊕	18
SPEED	🪶	4
ARMOR	⌗	16
FIREPOWER	🔥	18
SHOT LIMIT	⚡	13
VENOM	☠	0
JAW STRENGTH	💎	7
STEALTH	▤	5

Abilities: detecting the emotions of other dragons and Vikings, changing color based on mood

Personality: calm, sensitive

Other facts: Hobblegrunts turn yellow when they are content, purple when they are curious, and red when they are angry.

Terrible Terror
LOOKS CAN BE DECEIVING . . .

LENGTH: 1 ft 5 in	**WINGSPAN:** 6 ft 2 in	**WEIGHT:** 20 lbs

ATTACK	⊕	8
SPEED	✒	10
ARMOR	⌗	6
FIREPOWER	🔥	12
SHOT LIMIT	⚡	10
VENOM	💀	12
JAW STRENGTH	◆	2
STEALTH	☰	12

Abilities: singing songs, breathing surprisingly large flames from their small bodies

Personality: curious, mischievous

Other facts: Although each Terrible Terror is small in size, they become a threat when they travel in packs.

Fireworm

HOTTER THAN THE SUN

LENGTH: 2 in | **WINGSPAN:** 1/2 in | **WEIGHT:** 12 oz

ATTACK	⊕	4
SPEED	🪶	3
ARMOR	▦	5
FIREPOWER	🔥	30
SHOT LIMIT	⚡	2
VENOM	💀	0
JAW STRENGTH	💎	0
STEALTH	☰	6

Abilities: poisoning with a sting

Personality: not aggressive, but will become defensive when provoked

Other facts: Fireworms are the smallest of all dragons. They are controlled by a large Fireworm queen who lays thousands of eggs.

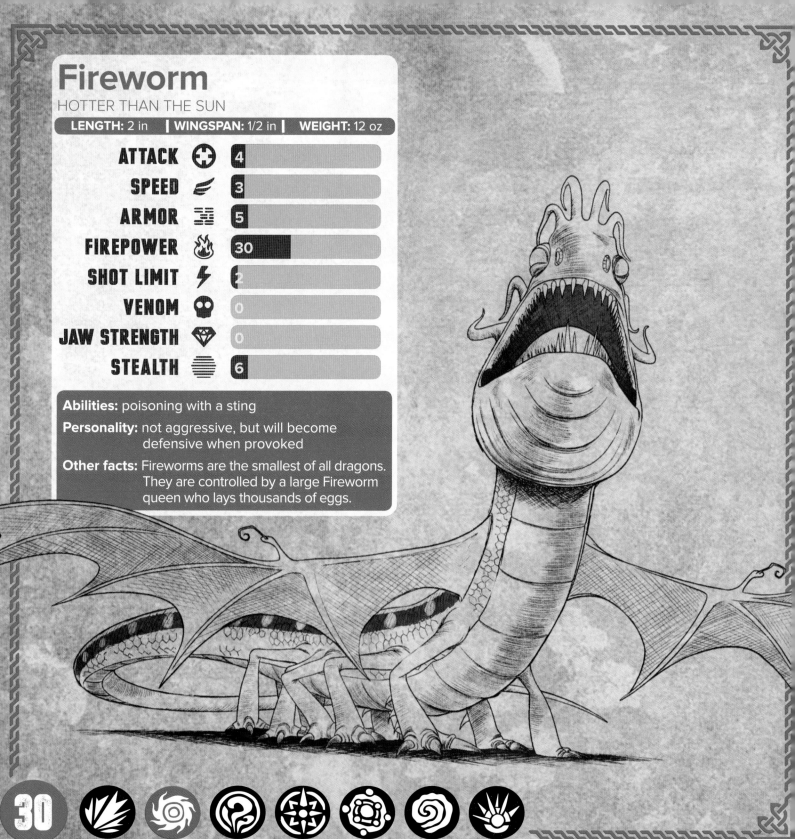

30

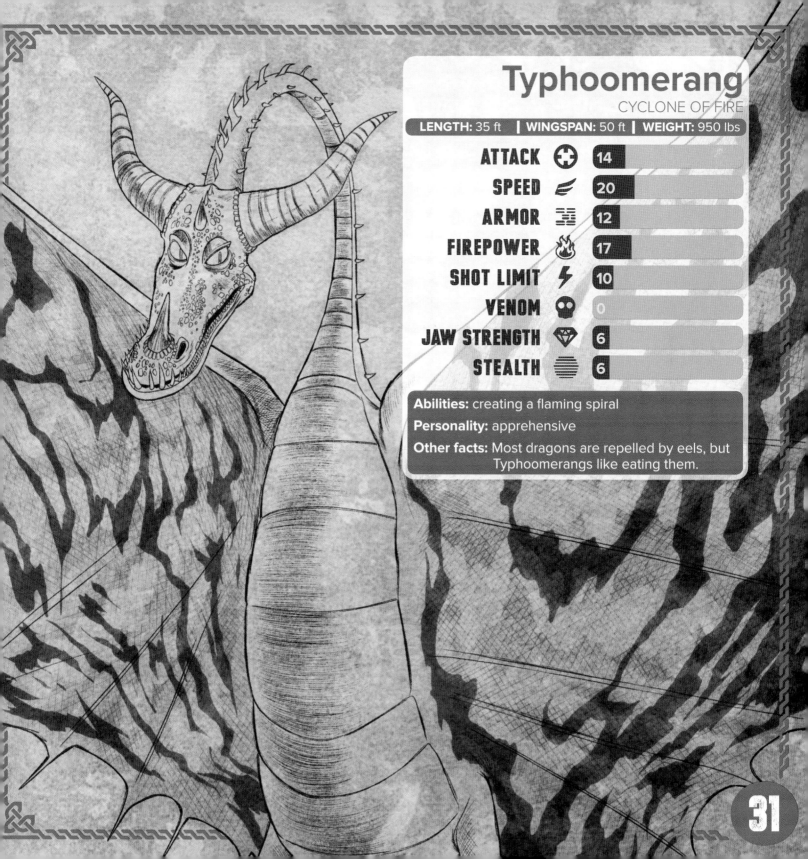

Typhoomerang
CYCLONE OF FIRE

LENGTH: 35 ft | **WINGSPAN:** 50 ft | **WEIGHT:** 950 lbs

ATTACK	⊕	14
SPEED	✦	20
ARMOR	⧉	12
FIREPOWER	🔥	17
SHOT LIMIT	⚡	10
VENOM	☠	0
JAW STRENGTH	◈	6
STEALTH	☰	6

Abilities: creating a flaming spiral

Personality: apprehensive

Other facts: Most dragons are repelled by eels, but Typhoomerangs like eating them.

31

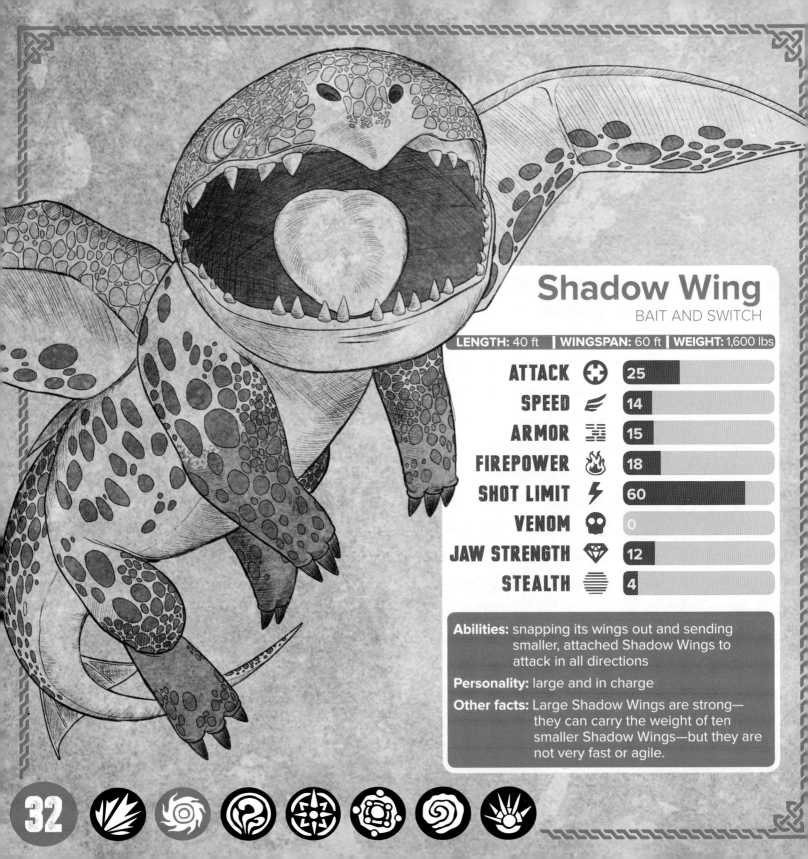

Shadow Wing

BAIT AND SWITCH

LENGTH: 40 ft | **WINGSPAN:** 60 ft | **WEIGHT:** 1,600 lbs

ATTACK	⊕	25
SPEED	✦	14
ARMOR	⋈	15
FIREPOWER	🔥	18
SHOT LIMIT	⚡	60
VENOM	☠	0
JAW STRENGTH	◆	12
STEALTH	⬢	4

Abilities: snapping its wings out and sending smaller, attached Shadow Wings to attack in all directions

Personality: large and in charge

Other facts: Large Shadow Wings are strong—they can carry the weight of ten smaller Shadow Wings—but they are not very fast or agile.

Night Terror
TRAVELING IN FLOCKS

LENGTH: 3 ft	WINGSPAN: 5 ft	WEIGHT: 14 lbs

Stat		Value
ATTACK		6
SPEED		6
ARMOR		4
FIREPOWER		10
SHOT LIMIT		5
VENOM		0
JAW STRENGTH		3
STEALTH		14

Abilities: flocking together to take the form of one larger dragon

Personality: shy but loyal

Other facts: A white, slightly larger Alpha Night Terror controls other Night Terrors. When threatened by an attack, the white Alpha organizes the others into a formidable flock.

33

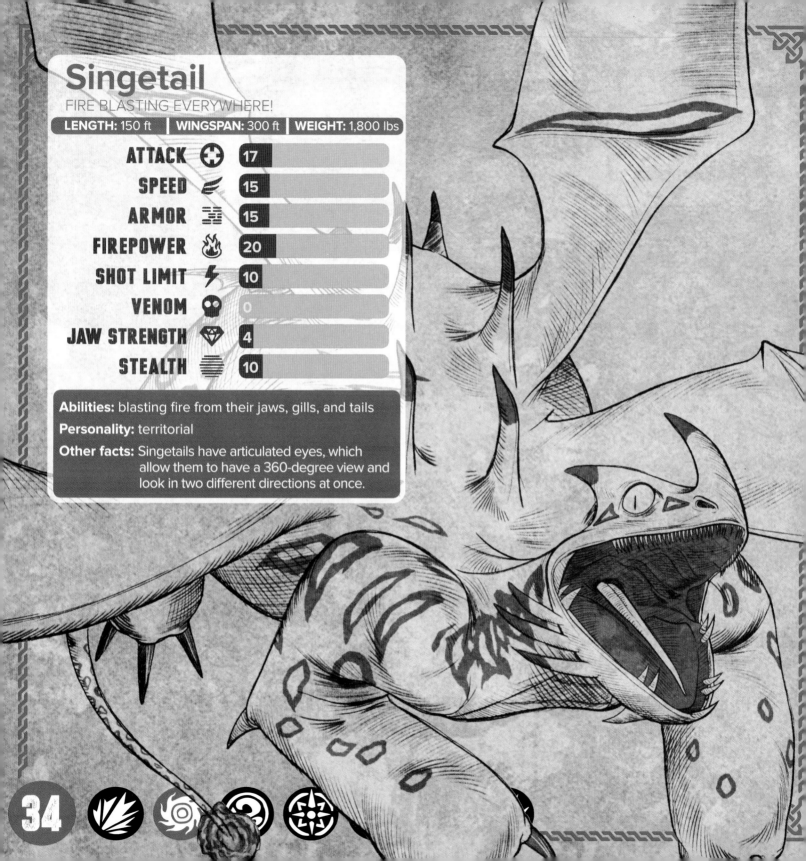

Singetail
FIRE BLASTING EVERYWHERE!

LENGTH: 150 ft | **WINGSPAN:** 300 ft | **WEIGHT:** 1,800 lbs

ATTACK	⊕	17
SPEED	🪶	15
ARMOR	⊠	15
FIREPOWER	🔥	20
SHOT LIMIT	⚡	10
VENOM	💀	0
JAW STRENGTH	💎	4
STEALTH	☰	10

Abilities: blasting fire from their jaws, gills, and tails

Personality: territorial

Other facts: Singetails have articulated eyes, which allow them to have a 360-degree view and look in two different directions at once.

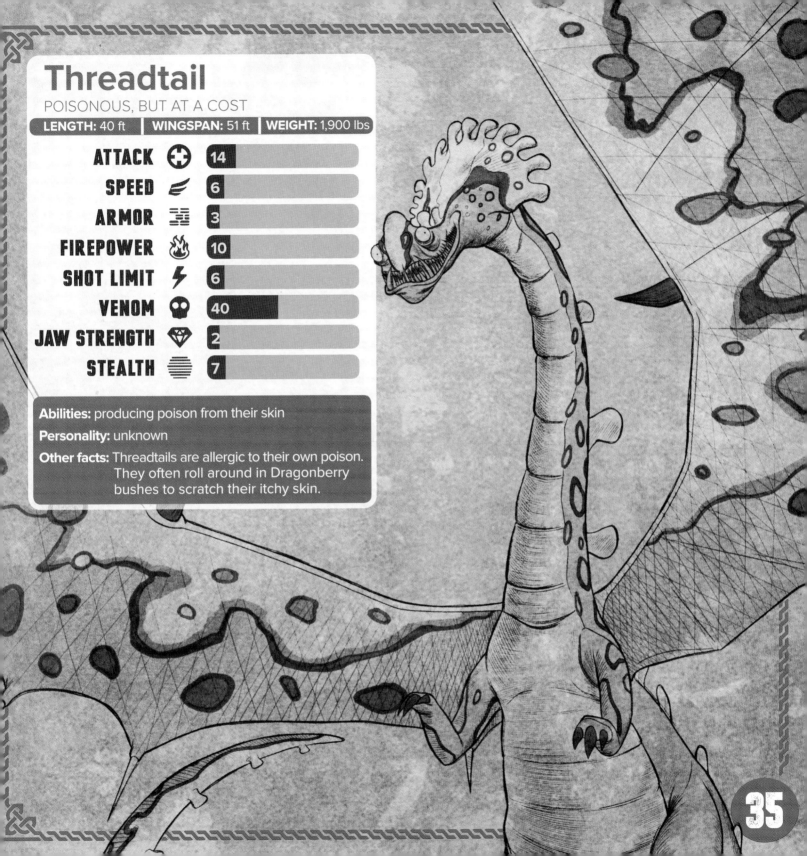

Threadtail
POISONOUS, BUT AT A COST

| LENGTH: 40 ft | WINGSPAN: 51 ft | WEIGHT: 1,900 lbs |

ATTACK	⊕	14
SPEED	🪶	6
ARMOR	▦	3
FIREPOWER	🔥	10
SHOT LIMIT	⚡	6
VENOM	💀	40
JAW STRENGTH	💎	2
STEALTH	▤	7

Abilities: producing poison from their skin

Personality: unknown

Other facts: Threadtails are allergic to their own poison. They often roll around in Dragonberry bushes to scratch their itchy skin.

MYSTERY CLASS

Shrouded in secrets, much is still unknown about Mystery Class dragons.

Hideous Zippleback
TWO HEADS ARE (MAYBE) BETTER THAN ONE

LENGTH: 66 ft	WINGSPAN: 38 ft	WEIGHT: 6,036 lbs

Stat		Value
ATTACK	✛	12
SPEED	🪽	10
ARMOR	☰	10
FIREPOWER	🔥	14
SHOT LIMIT	⚡	6
VENOM	💀	0
JAW STRENGTH	◈	6 (3 x 2)
STEALTH	≡	22 (11 x 2)

Abilities: one head breathing gas and the other head igniting it with a spark to create explosive fire

Personality: The different heads do not often get along or want to go in the same direction.

Other facts: Hideous Zipplebacks can transform into wheels of fire by creating their signature brand of fire, grabbing their tails, and spinning like bowling balls.

37

Flightmare PARALYZING GLOW

LENGTH: 30 ft	**WINGSPAN:** 50 ft	**WEIGHT:** 600 lbs

Stat		Value
ATTACK		10
SPEED		8
ARMOR		4
FIREPOWER		7
SHOT LIMIT		4
VENOM		10
JAW STRENGTH		4
STEALTH		7

Abilities: producing a temporarily paralyzing toxic mist

Personality: territorial, short-tempered

Other facts: Flightmares feed on algae that become luminous during Aurvandil's Fire. Eating the algae causes the Flightmares to glow, too.

Changewing MOODY CHAMELEON

LENGTH: 40 ft	WINGSPAN: 30 ft	WEIGHT: 950 lbs

ATTACK	9	
SPEED	14	
ARMOR	1	
FIREPOWER	12	
SHOT LIMIT	10	
VENOM	0	
JAW STRENGTH	2	
STEALTH	20	

Abilities: camouflaging; shooting hot acid that burns through wood and rocks

Personality: elusive, adaptable, agile

Other facts: Changewing eggs are smooth and iridescent. Vikings sometimes mistake them for gemstones.

Death Song
SO BEAUTIFUL, IT'S HYPNOTIC

LENGTH: 75 ft	WINGSPAN: 85 ft	WEIGHT: 1,200 lbs

Stat		Value
ATTACK		16
SPEED		17
ARMOR		16
FIREPOWER		13
SHOT LIMIT		8
VENOM		0
JAW STRENGTH		10
STEALTH		0

Abilities: luring dragons with a hypnotic siren and trapping them

Personality: solitary

Other facts: Death Songs trap victims by shooting out a thick liquid that quickly solidifies into a hard amber-like cocoon. The cocoon can only be penetrated by fire.

43

Smothering Smokebreath

CLOAKED IN SMOKE

LENGTH: 6 ft	WINGSPAN: 10 ft	WEIGHT: 140 lbs

ATTACK	6	SHOT LIMIT	3
SPEED	8	VENOM	0
ARMOR	6	JAW STRENGTH	8
FIREPOWER	6	STEALTH	15

Abilities: exhaling plumes of thick, black smoke (rather than fire) to disorient enemies

Personality: stealthy, territorial

Other facts: Smothering Smokebreaths make their nests out of metal scraps.

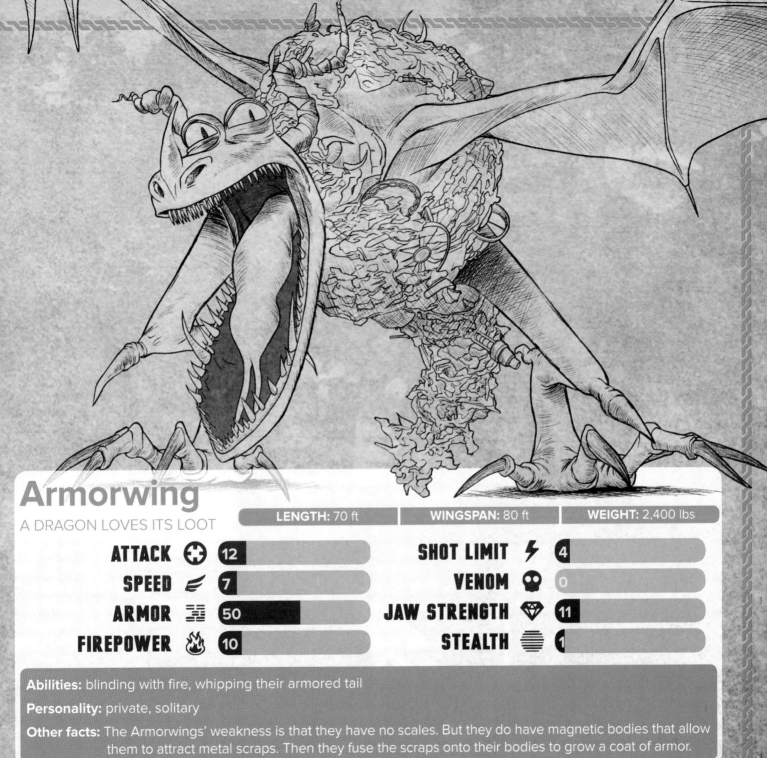

Armorwing
A DRAGON LOVES ITS LOOT

LENGTH: 70 ft	WINGSPAN: 80 ft	WEIGHT: 2,400 lbs

ATTACK	12	SHOT LIMIT	4
SPEED	7	VENOM	0
ARMOR	50	JAW STRENGTH	11
FIREPOWER	10	STEALTH	1

Abilities: blinding with fire, whipping their armored tail

Personality: private, solitary

Other facts: The Armorwings' weakness is that they have no scales. But they do have magnetic bodies that allow them to attract metal scraps. Then they fuse the scraps onto their bodies to grow a coat of armor.

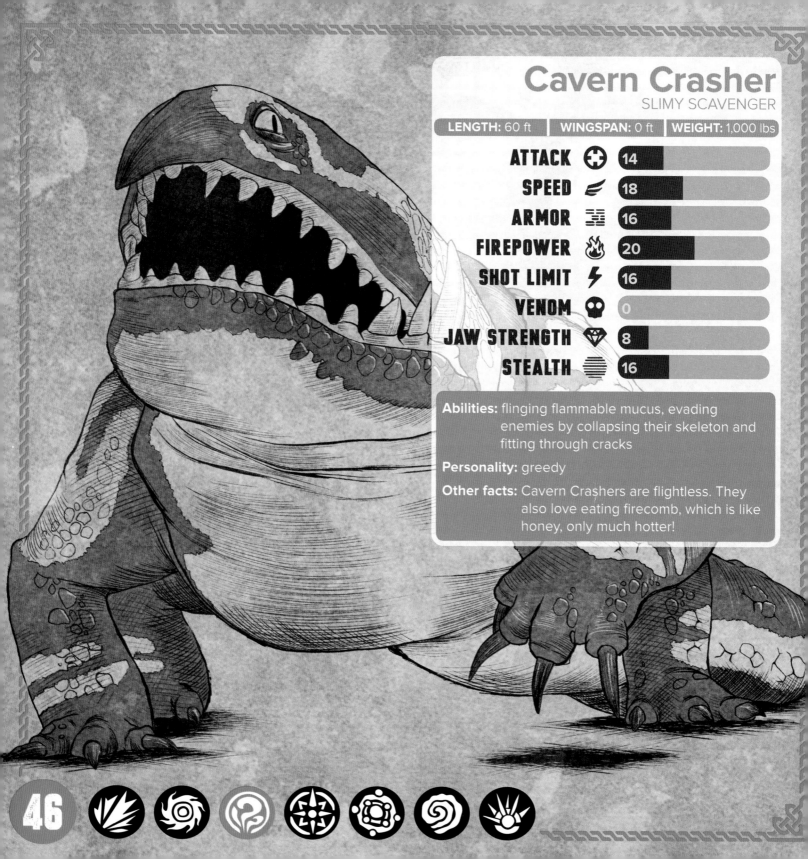

Cavern Crasher
SLIMY SCAVENGER

LENGTH: 60 ft	WINGSPAN: 0 ft	WEIGHT: 1,000 lbs

ATTACK		14
SPEED		18
ARMOR		16
FIREPOWER		20
SHOT LIMIT		16
VENOM		0
JAW STRENGTH		8
STEALTH		16

Abilities: flinging flammable mucus, evading enemies by collapsing their skeleton and fitting through cracks

Personality: greedy

Other facts: Cavern Crashers are flightless. They also love eating firecomb, which is like honey, only much hotter!

Slitherwing
TOXIC TO THE TOUCH

LENGTH: 40 ft	WINGSPAN: 60 ft	WEIGHT: 1,000 lbs

ATTACK	⊕	14
SPEED	🪽	18
ARMOR	⋈	13
FIREPOWER	🔥	0
SHOT LIMIT	⚡	0
VENOM	☠	20
JAW STRENGTH	💎	8
STEALTH	▤	9

Abilities: poisoning with their venomous scales and fangs, hunting in packs

Personality: aggressive

Other facts: The more colorful a Slitherwing, the more poisonous it is.

Snaptrapper
VENUS FLYTRAP OF DRAGONS

LENGTH: 68 ft	WINGSPAN: 35 ft	WEIGHT: 5,800 lbs

ATTACK	⊕	10	**SHOT LIMIT**	⚡	4
SPEED	🪶	4	**VENOM**	💀	18
ARMOR	🗒	4	**JAW STRENGTH**	💎	28 (7 x 4)
FIREPOWER	🔥	6	**STEALTH**	▦	60 (15 x 4)

Abilities: baiting prey by emitting sweet scents, then trapping them in their triple-split jaws

Personality: patient

Other facts: Snaptrappers can produce a terribly unpleasant odor to scare off predators.

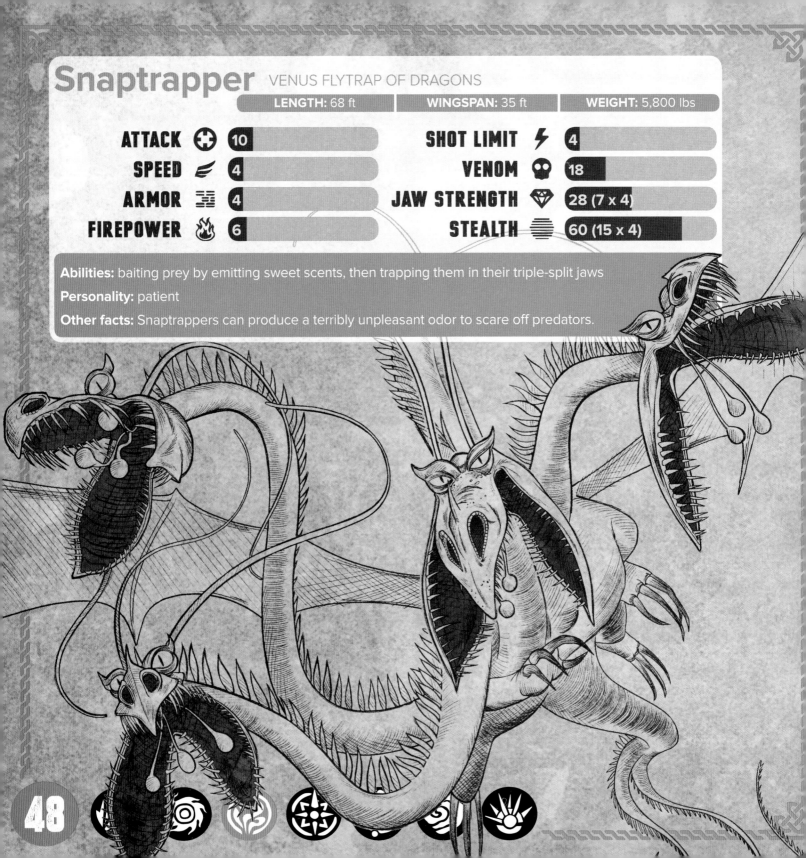

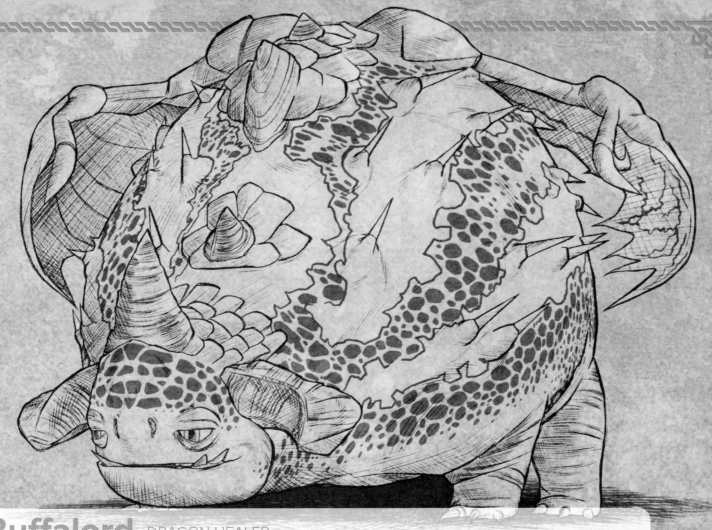

Buffalord DRAGON HEALER

LENGTH: 30 ft	WINGSPAN: 50 ft	WEIGHT: 950 lbs

ATTACK	⊕	8	SHOT LIMIT	⚡	6
SPEED	🪽	6	VENOM	💀	-20 (healing)
ARMOR	⚏	16	JAW STRENGTH	💎	6
FIREPOWER	🔥	12	STEALTH	☰	4

Abilities: curing the Scourge of Odin (a deadly disease), firing spikes

Personality: kind-hearted, peaceful

Other facts: Buffalords can puff up to double their original size, causing any dragon hunters to think twice before approaching.

Dramillion
PARROT OF THE DRAGON WORLD

| LENGTH: 20 ft | WINGSPAN: 35 ft | WEIGHT: 600 lbs |

ATTACK	18
SPEED	14
ARMOR	8
FIREPOWER	20
SHOT LIMIT	40
VENOM	0
JAW STRENGTH	6
STEALTH	8

Abilities: copying and repeating other dragons' fire blasts

Personality: imitative

Other facts: Compared to other dragons, Dramillions can blast the most amount of fire before burning out. They can also transfer flames to each other.

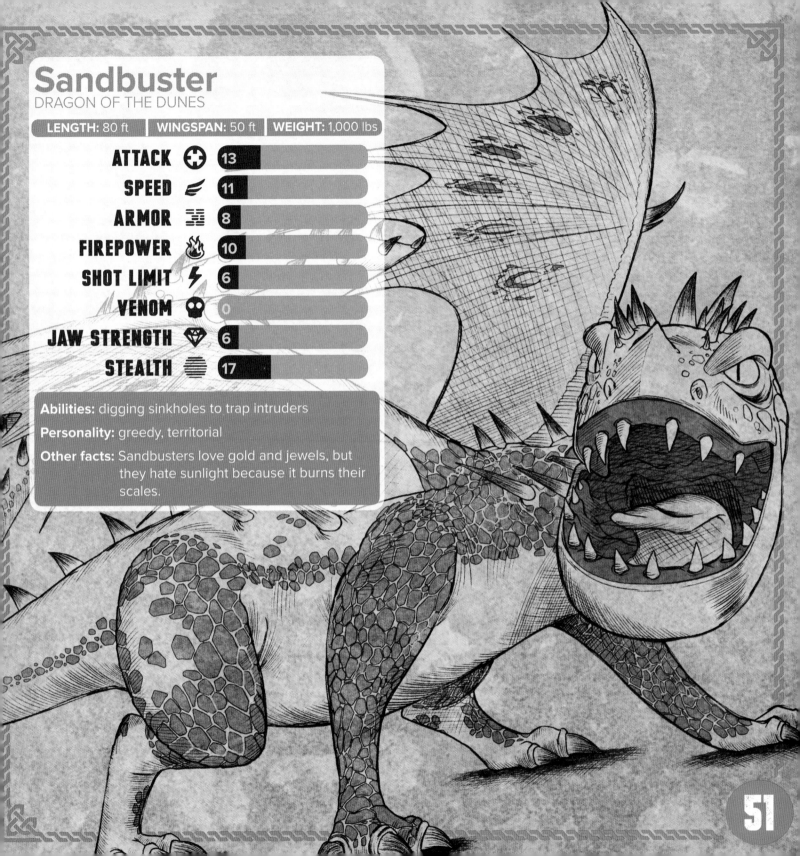

Sandbuster
DRAGON OF THE DUNES

LENGTH: 80 ft | **WINGSPAN:** 50 ft | **WEIGHT:** 1,000 lbs

ATTACK	✛	13
SPEED	🪶	11
ARMOR	☰	8
FIREPOWER	🔥	10
SHOT LIMIT	⚡	6
VENOM	💀	0
JAW STRENGTH	💎	6
STEALTH	▤	17

Abilities: digging sinkholes to trap intruders

Personality: greedy, territorial

Other facts: Sandbusters love gold and jewels, but they hate sunlight because it burns their scales.

TRACKER CLASS

Above the clouds, under the waterfalls, inside the Hidden World . . . Tracker Class dragons can pinpoint any Viking or dragon with astounding accuracy.

Deadly Nadder — LETHAL BEAUTY

LENGTH: 30 ft	WINGSPAN: 42 ft	WEIGHT: 2,628 lbs

ATTACK	10
SPEED	8
ARMOR	16
FIREPOWER	18
SHOT LIMIT	6
VENOM	16
JAW STRENGTH	5
STEALTH	10

Abilities: shooting spikes from their hides and tails, tracking scents

Personality: fastidious, playful

Other facts: The Deadly Nadder's magnesium fire is the hottest of any dragon.

Rumblehorn BLOODHOUND OF DRAGONS

LENGTH: 11 ft 1/2 in	WINGSPAN: 30 ft	WEIGHT: 1,100 lbs

ATTACK		11
SPEED		7
ARMOR		12
FIREPOWER		22
SHOT LIMIT		4
VENOM		0
JAW STRENGTH		5
STEALTH		6

Abilities: ramming with their ax-shaped heads, tracking scents

Personality: intelligent, stealthy, flexible

Other facts: Rumblehorns are so heavy that they can tip over a ship while flying at full speed.

Windgnasher
TRACKING THROUGH THE ARCHIPELAGO AND BEYOND

LENGTH: 25 ft	WINGSPAN: 30 ft	WEIGHT: 2000 lbs

ATTACK	14	
SPEED	16	
ARMOR	18	
FIREPOWER	9	
SHOT LIMIT	16	
VENOM	0	
JAW STRENGTH	18	
STEALTH	10	

Abilities: thrashing its mace-like tail, tracking scents

Personality: reliable

Other facts: During battle, Windgnashers like to fire from the back of the pack.

BOULDER CLASS

Loyal defenders of the earth, Boulder Class dragons will do anything—from spewing lava to blasting the bumps off their rugged exteriors—in order to protect their land and their friends.

Gronckle SOLID AS A ROCK

LENGTH: 14 ft	WINGSPAN: 18 ft	WEIGHT: 5,724 lbs

ATTACK	✚	8
SPEED	✦	4
ARMOR	☰	20
FIREPOWER	🔥	14
SHOT LIMIT	⚡	6
VENOM	💀	0
JAW STRENGTH	◈	8
STEALTH	☰	5

Abilities: shooting flaming chunks of rock and lava

Personality: sweet, sensitive, and cautious

Other facts: Gronckles are the only dragons that can fly backward and sideways.

Crimson Goregutter ANTLERS THAT BLAZE

LENGTH: 30 ft	WINGSPAN: 24 ft	WEIGHT: 2,500 lbs

Stat		Value
ATTACK		17
SPEED		10
ARMOR		18
FIREPOWER		12
SHOT LIMIT		6
VENOM		0
JAW STRENGTH		12
STEALTH		13

Abilities: covering their antlers with lava before attacking, producing an ear-splitting call

Personality: shy, but noisy when they need to be!

Other facts: Crimson Goregutters prefer to stay alone rather than seek out the company of dragons or Vikings.

Hotburple

"LARGE, SNORING OAF OF A DRAGON"
—GOBBER

LENGTH: 14 ft	WINGSPAN: 18 ft	WEIGHT: 5,724 lbs

Stat		Value
ATTACK		8
SPEED		4
ARMOR		20
FIREPOWER		14
SHOT LIMIT		6
VENOM		0
JAW STRENGTH		8
STEALTH		5

Abilities: shooting flaming chunks of rock and lava

Personality: lazy, fussy, difficult to keep awake

Other facts: Hotburples sometimes fall asleep while flying in midair.

Whispering Death
UNDERGROUND MENACE

LENGTH: 50 ft	WINGSPAN: 10 ft	WEIGHT: 2,000 lbs

Stat		Value
ATTACK		8
SPEED		7
ARMOR		7
FIREPOWER		3
SHOT LIMIT		1
VENOM		2
JAW STRENGTH		4
STEALTH		10

Abilities: inhaling deeply to create a powerful vacuum, boring through solid material with their drill-like teeth, creating a rumbling whisper that precedes their attack

Personality: intelligent

Other facts: Whispering Deaths prefer being on the ground rather than flying.

65

Screaming Death

RED-EYED NIGHTMARE

LENGTH: 50 ft	WINGSPAN: 10 ft	WEIGHT: 2,500 lbs

ATTACK ✦ **16**

SPEED ⟩ **8**

ARMOR ▥ **20**

FIREPOWER 🔥 **10**

SHOT LIMIT ⚡ **2**

VENOM 💀 **10**

JAW STRENGTH ◈ **11**

STEALTH ▤ **14**

Abilities: shooting spines from their tails, breathing massive amounts of fire in a single blast, burrowing underground, disorienting others with their screams

Personality: angry, powerful

Other facts: Born once every hundred years or so, the Screaming Death has all the strengths of the Whispering Death with none of its weaknesses.

Catastrophic Quaken SEISMIC GIANT

LENGTH: 30 ft	WINGSPAN: 8 ft	WEIGHT: 2,500 lbs

ATTACK	12
SPEED	14
ARMOR	35
FIREPOWER	10
SHOT LIMIT	6
VENOM	0
JAW STRENGTH	20
STEALTH	3

Abilities: spewing out molten rock, smashing the ground to create shock waves

Personality: cautious

Other facts: A Catastrophic Quaken can curl up into a ball like a huge armadillo to defend itself.

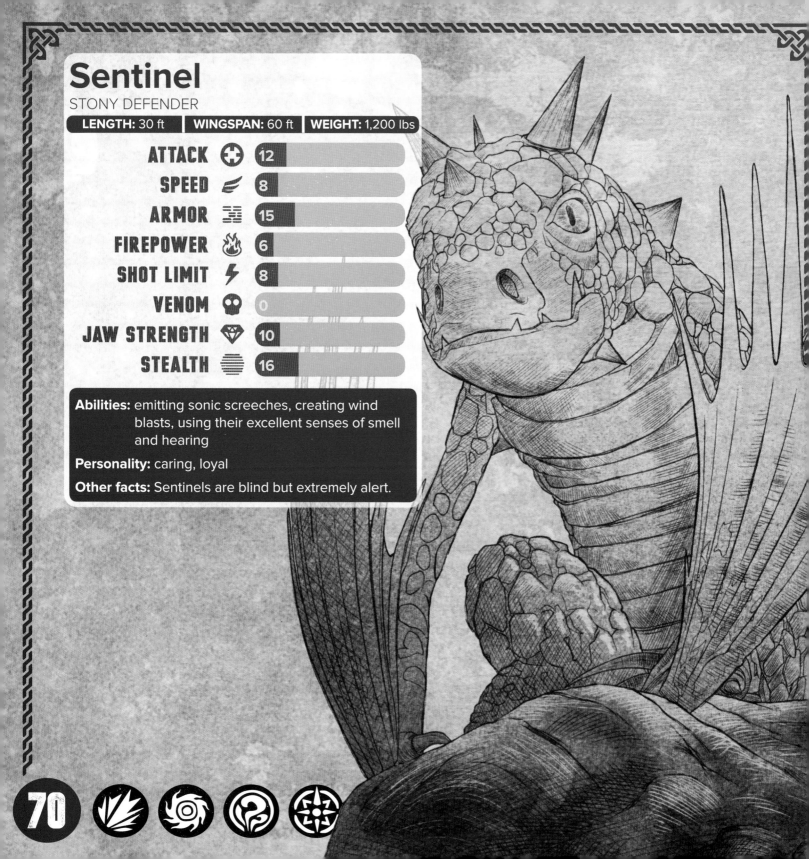

Sentinel
STONY DEFENDER

LENGTH: 30 ft | **WINGSPAN:** 60 ft | **WEIGHT:** 1,200 lbs

Stat	Value
ATTACK	12
SPEED	8
ARMOR	15
FIREPOWER	6
SHOT LIMIT	8
VENOM	0
JAW STRENGTH	10
STEALTH	16

Abilities: emitting sonic screeches, creating wind blasts, using their excellent senses of smell and hearing

Personality: caring, loyal

Other facts: Sentinels are blind but extremely alert.

70

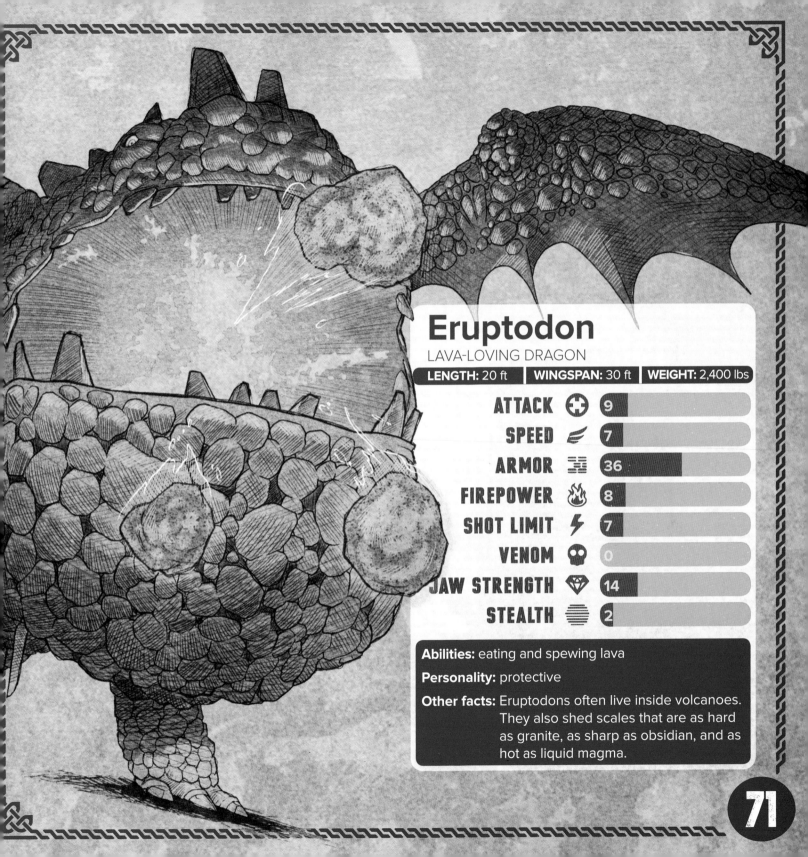

Eruptodon

LAVA-LOVING DRAGON

LENGTH: 20 ft	WINGSPAN: 30 ft	WEIGHT: 2,400 lbs

ATTACK	9
SPEED	7
ARMOR	36
FIREPOWER	8
SHOT LIMIT	7
VENOM	0
JAW STRENGTH	14
STEALTH	2

Abilities: eating and spewing lava

Personality: protective

Other facts: Eruptodons often live inside volcanoes. They also shed scales that are as hard as granite, as sharp as obsidian, and as hot as liquid magma.

Snafflefang
BITING, CHOMPING, GNAWING

LENGTH: 30 ft	**WINGSPAN:** 40 ft	**WEIGHT:** 2,814 lbs

Stat		Value
ATTACK	✛	9
SPEED	🪽	5
ARMOR	▤	17
FIREPOWER	🔥	13
SHOT LIMIT	⚡	6
VENOM	💀	12
JAW STRENGTH	💎	8
STEALTH	▤	8

Abilities: shooting crystal-flecked fireballs, swinging spiky tails for defense or attack

Personality: active, watchful, gentle

Other facts: Snafflefangs like to gnaw on geodes with their sharp teeth.

Shovelhelm

BUILDER OF THE DRAGON WORLD

| LENGTH: 30 ft | WINGSPAN: 40 ft | WEIGHT: 3,500 lbs |

ATTACK	⊕	10
SPEED	⪜	5
ARMOR	▤	20
FIREPOWER	🔥	10
SHOT LIMIT	⚡	6
VENOM	💀	8
JAW STRENGTH	💎	16
STEALTH	▤	8

Abilities: digging with their scooping chins, hammering with their hard heads

Personality: observant, helpful

Other facts: Instead of charging straight into battle, Shovelhelms like to stand back and evaluate the situation first. That way, they can figure out the best way to fight.

73

TIDAL CLASS

Tidal Class dragons reign over the sea, often causing fear in their wake.

Bewilderbeast
KIND-HEARTED PROTECTOR

LENGTH: 520 ft	WINGSPAN: 150 ft	WEIGHT: 100 tons (200,000 lbs)

ATTACK	✛	50
SPEED	⚘	6 on land, 18 underwater
ARMOR	⛉	38
FIREPOWER	🔥	60
SHOT LIMIT	⚡	8
VENOM	☠	0
JAW STRENGTH	💎	48
STEALTH	☰	2

Abilities: blasting massive sprays of ice, intimidating others with their size

Personality: kind and docile, ruling all dragons without harm

Other facts: Bewilderbeasts are the biggest sea dragons.

Thunderdrum SOUND OF THE SEA

LENGTH: 68 ft	WINGSPAN: 48 ft	WEIGHT: 900 lbs

ATTACK		12
SPEED		14
ARMOR		10
FIREPOWER		16
SHOT LIMIT		6
VENOM		0
JAW STRENGTH		7
STEALTH		8

Abilities: expanding its mouth to blast sonic booms

Personality: headstrong, loyal

Other facts: By changing the frequency of its roars, a Thunderdrum can cancel out another Thunderdrum's sonic blasts, thereby neutralizing an attack.

Scauldron
BUBBLING AND BOILING

LENGTH: 65 ft	WINGSPAN: 75 ft	WEIGHT: 3,000 lbs

Stat		Value
ATTACK		10
SPEED		6
ARMOR		6
FIREPOWER		14
SHOT LIMIT		14
VENOM		10 for Vikings, -10 for dragons
JAW STRENGTH		4
STEALTH		10

Abilities: blasting boiling hot water

Personality: aggressive, predatory, travels in pods

Other facts: The Scauldron's venom is the only known antidote to Blue Oleander flowers, which are poisonous to dragons.

Seashocker DOUBLE-HEADED SEA DWELLER

LENGTH: 52 ft	WINGSPAN: 50 ft	WEIGHT: 2,200 lbs

Stat		Value
ATTACK	✛	18
SPEED	✦	16
ARMOR	▦	20
FIREPOWER	🔥	7
SHOT LIMIT	⚡	12 (6 x 2)
VENOM	☠	14
JAW STRENGTH	◈	8 (4 x 2)
STEALTH	▬	10

Abilities: emitting underwater sonar rather than breathing fire, paralyzing victims with electrical charges, cutting through sheets of ice with their dense dorsal fins

Personality: stealthy, predatory

Other facts: Seashocker dorsal fins are made of incredibly dense cartilage, which allows them to cut through frozen ice fields and reach ice-bound prey.

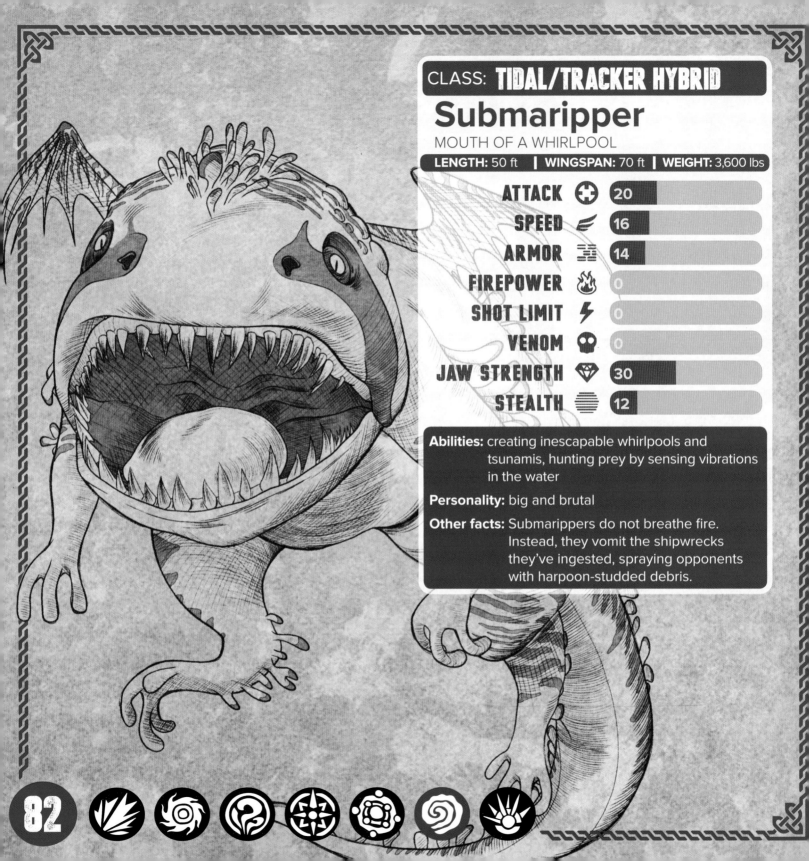

CLASS: TIDAL/TRACKER HYBRID

Submaripper
MOUTH OF A WHIRLPOOL

LENGTH: 50 ft | **WINGSPAN:** 70 ft | **WEIGHT:** 3,600 lbs

ATTACK	✛	20
SPEED	🪽	16
ARMOR	▦	14
FIREPOWER	🔥	0
SHOT LIMIT	⚡	0
VENOM	☠	0
JAW STRENGTH	💎	30
STEALTH	▤	12

Abilities: creating inescapable whirlpools and tsunamis, hunting prey by sensing vibrations in the water

Personality: big and brutal

Other facts: Submarippers do not breathe fire. Instead, they vomit the shipwrecks they've ingested, spraying opponents with harpoon-studded debris.

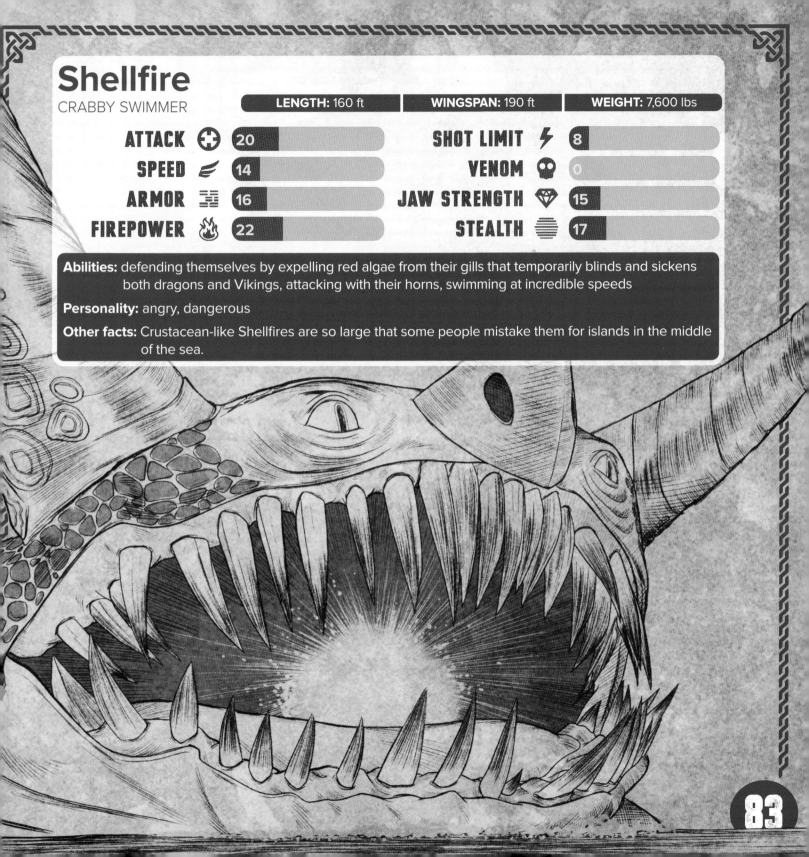

Shellfire
CRABBY SWIMMER

LENGTH: 160 ft	WINGSPAN: 190 ft	WEIGHT: 7,600 lbs

ATTACK	20	SHOT LIMIT	8
SPEED	14	VENOM	0
ARMOR	16	JAW STRENGTH	15
FIREPOWER	22	STEALTH	17

Abilities: defending themselves by expelling red algae from their gills that temporarily blinds and sickens both dragons and Vikings, attacking with their horns, swimming at incredible speeds

Personality: angry, dangerous

Other facts: Crustacean-like Shellfires are so large that some people mistake them for islands in the middle of the sea.

SHARP CLASS

Sharp Class dragons have razor-sharp minds and razor-sharp wings and tails!

Stormcutter FOUR-WINGED FORCE OF NATURE

LENGTH: 31 ft 3 1/4 in | **WINGSPAN:** 48 ft (diagonally) | **WEIGHT:** 2,500 lbs

Stat	Value
ATTACK	10
SPEED	17
ARMOR	4
FIREPOWER	12
SHOT LIMIT	8
VENOM	0
JAW STRENGTH	5
STEALTH	13

Abilities: X-wing flying, shooting fire in a spiral shape

Personality: intelligent, playful, sensitive, powerful

Other facts: Stormcutters have two sets of wings, allowing them to brake in midair.

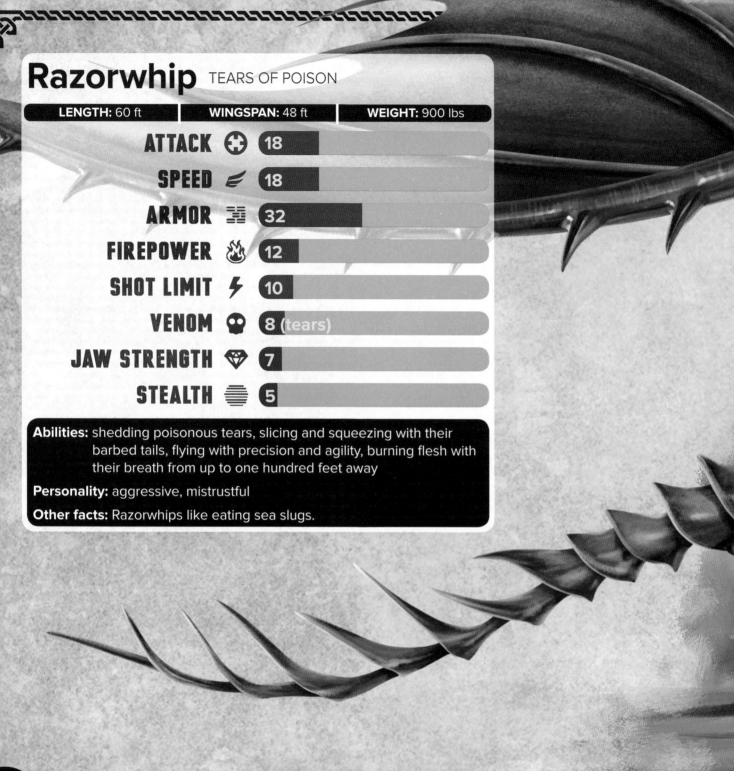

Razorwhip TEARS OF POISON

LENGTH: 60 ft	WINGSPAN: 48 ft	WEIGHT: 900 lbs

ATTACK	18
SPEED	18
ARMOR	32
FIREPOWER	12
SHOT LIMIT	10
VENOM	8 (tears)
JAW STRENGTH	7
STEALTH	5

Abilities: shedding poisonous tears, slicing and squeezing with their barbed tails, flying with precision and agility, burning flesh with their breath from up to one hundred feet away

Personality: aggressive, mistrustful

Other facts: Razorwhips like eating sea slugs.

Timberjack   WINGS THAT SLICE

LENGTH: 60 ft	WINGSPAN: 90 ft	WEIGHT: 900 lbs

ATTACK	10	
SPEED	12	
ARMOR	8	
FIREPOWER	10	
SHOT LIMIT	8	
VENOM	0	
JAW STRENGTH	3	
STEALTH	13	

Abilities: slicing with razor-sharp wings, creating tentlike shelters with their wings for weary riders and smaller dragons

Personality: sensitive, protective

Other facts: Timberjack wings can slice through the thickest tree trunks without slowing their flight.

Speed Stinger
FASTEST DRAGONS ON LAND

LENGTH: 16 ft	WINGSPAN: Flightless	WEIGHT: 600 lbs

ATTACK	12	SHOT LIMIT	0
SPEED	30	VENOM	15
ARMOR	10	JAW STRENGTH	5
FIREPOWER	0	STEALTH	30

Abilities: coordinating attacks, temporarily paralyzing dragons and Vikings with their poisonous barbed tails

Personality: aggressive, intelligent, conspiring

Other facts: Speed Stingers are the fastest runners on land. They are also nocturnal. The Alpha Speed Stinger is identifiable by its red fins and red stripes.

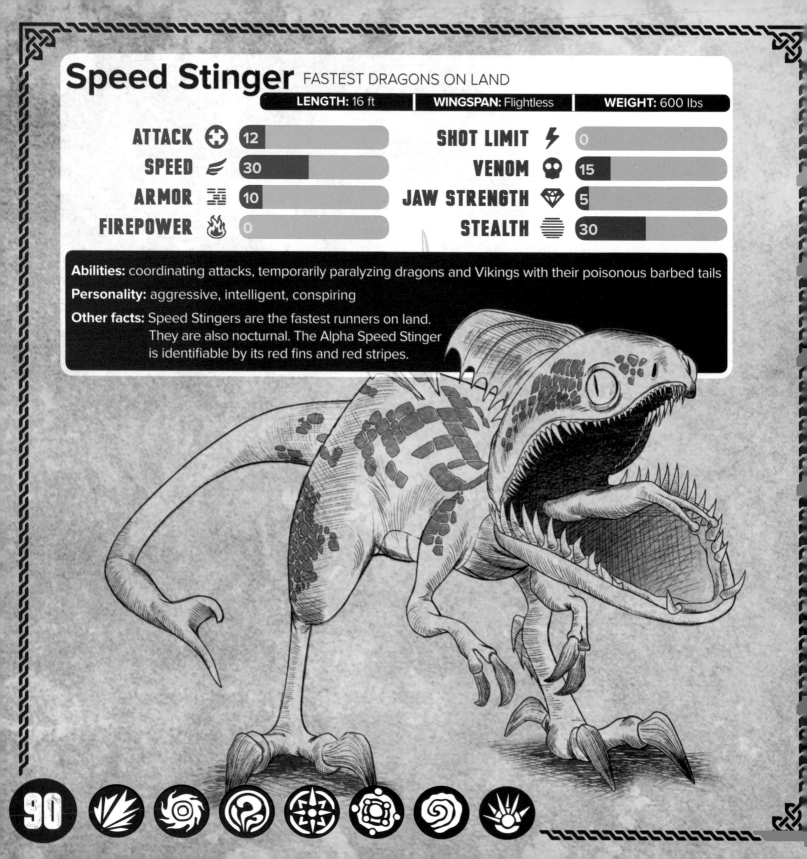

Scuttleclaw

WILD AND FREE

LENGTH: 18 ft	WINGSPAN: 20 ft	WEIGHT: 600 lbs

ATTACK	10	SHOT LIMIT	8
SPEED	16	VENOM	2
ARMOR	8	JAW STRENGTH	3
FIREPOWER	10	STEALTH	10

Abilities: naturally resisting Alpha control (as a baby)

Personality: restless, wild

Other facts: Baby Scuttleclaws are extremely active and difficult to control.

Grim Gnasher
TOOTHY DRAGON VULTURES

LENGTH: 10 ft | **WINGSPAN:** 14 ft | **WEIGHT:** 400 lbs

ATTACK	✛	10
SPEED	🪽	12
ARMOR	䷀	7
FIREPOWER	🔥	9
SHOT LIMIT	⚡	5
VENOM	💀	0
JAW STRENGTH	💎	12
STEALTH	☰	7

Abilities: regenerating rows of teeth, spitting out blasts of sharp fangs

Personality: sneaky, smart, opportunistic

Other facts: Grim Gnashers travel in pods and like to hunt weaker dragons. They are also immune to Slitherwing venom.

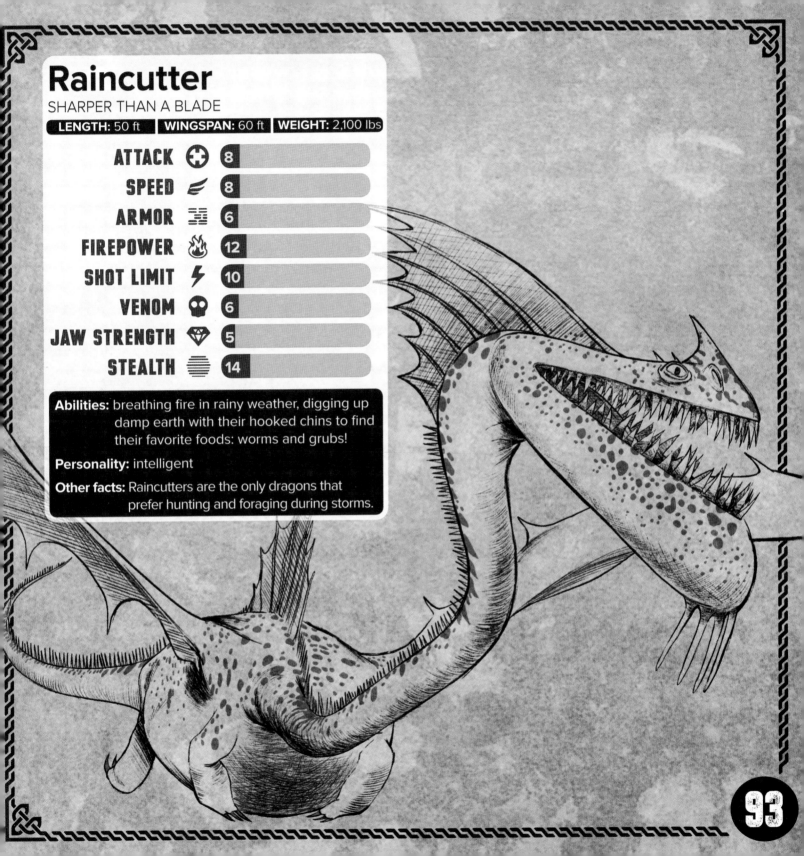

Raincutter

SHARPER THAN A BLADE

| LENGTH: 50 ft | WINGSPAN: 60 ft | WEIGHT: 2,100 lbs |

ATTACK	✛	8
SPEED	✎	8
ARMOR	▤	6
FIREPOWER	🔥	12
SHOT LIMIT	⚡	10
VENOM	💀	6
JAW STRENGTH	💎	5
STEALTH	▤	14

Abilities: breathing fire in rainy weather, digging up damp earth with their hooked chins to find their favorite foods: worms and grubs!

Personality: intelligent

Other facts: Raincutters are the only dragons that prefer hunting and foraging during storms.

THE HIDDEN WORLD IS A VAST KINGDOM,

far more expansive than you can navigate at once. As you proceed on your journey, we trust that you'll safeguard all that you've discovered—and will continue to discover—about the dragons and their secret world. It is up to you to protect these magnificent creatures from dragon trappers.

A final message before we part: whenever you see lava spewing from the earth, think of the dragons. They may be reminding you that they are still living under the ground, flourishing in the Hidden World . . . and waiting for the day when humans and dragons can live together in peace.